Where Is Gus-Gus?

by Claire Daniel
illustrated by Jamie Smith

HOUGHTON MIFFLIN HARCOURT
School Publishers

Printed in China

ISBN-13: 978-0-547-01662-7
ISBN-10: 0-547-01662-X

4 5 6 7 8 0940 18 17 16 15 14 13 12 11 10

One Saturday morning, I was sleeping. Suddenly, I heard something I did not want to hear.

Mom's voice boomed, "Wake up, Bernie!"

I groaned. "But it's the weekend. I want to sleep."

"Bernie!" she insisted. "We're going to see Grandma today. Remember?"

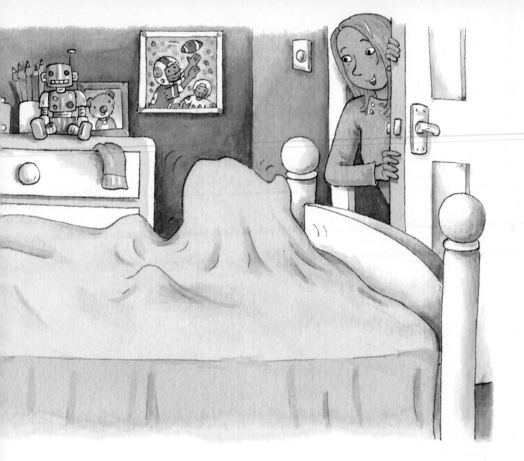

I did remember. My friends and I were going to visit Grandma at the Gentle Creek Home. We were all bringing our pets.

My dog Oscar was ready to go even if I wasn't.

"Where is Gus-Gus?" I asked. "I want to bring my puppy to Grandma's too."

"Gus-Gus will show up, Bernie," Mom said. "You get dressed and get ready for breakfast."

Gus-Gus must have heard the word *breakfast*.
His head popped out from under the blankets
on my bed. He loved to sleep under the covers
with me.

I hugged my puppy. He sprinkled my face with
wet kisses. One day Gus-Gus would look just like
Oscar. For now, he was just a little puppy who
always got lost!

After breakfast, my friends and I arrived at the Gentle Creek Home. All of us had brought our pets. Wes had his rabbit, and Maribel had her hamster. Andy had his cat, and Simon had his monkey.

We all gathered in the living room with Grandma and her friends. Grandma was excited to see me, but I'm not so sure she was happy to see Simon's monkey!

Everything was going great until the pets noticed one another. Then the rabbit started chasing the hamster, and the cat started chasing the rabbit. Oscar was not about to miss the fun. He ran after the cat! Simon's monkey shrieked at the other pets.

We all yelled at our pets to stop chasing one another, but I don't think they heard us. There were noises coming from everywhere. Soon I started laughing. Then all my friends were bursting out laughing, too.

STOP!

Finally, things got really crazy. Then
Grandma bellowed, "Stop!" All the pets listened
to her and stopped chasing one another. Even
Simon's monkey became quiet.

Grandma took a deep breath and smiled. Then
she said, "It is so wonderful that everyone brought
their pets. But they have to be quieter and calmer.
What if we pretend like we're at your school?
Think about how you share things at school. Let's
do the same with your pets. You can show them to
us one at a time."

I put Oscar on a leash. Wes put his pet rabbit in a box, and Maribel put her hamster in a cage. Andy held his cat in a cat carrier, and Simon made sure his monkey sat on a chair and did not move. Then we took turns sharing our pets with Grandma and her friends.

Oscar and I waited for our turn. That's when I noticed that my puppy Gus-Gus was missing. I looked at Mom. She had just been holding him on a leash. "Where is Gus-Gus?" I whispered to her.

Suddenly, Mom looked surprised and a little worried. For a short moment, everyone was quiet. And everyone heard Mom whisper to Grandma, "Where is Gus-Gus?"

Everyone looked for Gus-Gus. Wes and his rabbit looked under the chairs in the living room, but Gus-Gus was not there. Andy and his cat looked in the kitchen, but Gus-Gus was not there. Maribel and her hamster looked in the garden, but Gus-Gus was not there either. Simon's monkey looked everywhere that was up high. He checked the tops of all the closets and bookshelves. He even climbed the trees outside.

No one could find Gus-Gus! Grandma was getting tired. "I need to take a nap," she said. "Don't worry about Gus-Gus. I'm sure you will find him."

Mom and Grandma went to her room. Everyone else kept looking for Gus-Gus. Then Mom came back into the living room. She had a big smile on her face.

"How can you be happy when Gus-Gus is lost?" I asked.

"I'm sure Gus-Gus is fine," she said. "Grandma wants a kiss from you before she falls asleep."

Grandma was almost asleep when I reached
her bed. But I noticed that she was smiling, too. I
leaned over to kiss her and that's when I noticed
the small lump in her bed.

It was a very strange lump! I touched the lump
and it moved. The lump moved toward the edge
of the bed, so I lifted the covers. Gus-Gus looked
up at me and licked my face! He had been hiding
under the covers again!

Gus-Gus was not lost anymore! Everyone came into Grandma's room. Wes's rabbit hopped into the room, and Maribel's hamster snuggled in her arms. Andy's cat purred, and Simon's monkey clapped.

"I think it's wonderful you have friends," said Grandma. "I think it's wonderful that your friends have pets, too."

"Pets teach us how to love," said Grandma. "They even remind us to laugh." She petted Gus-Gus.

"Does this mean that we can come to see you again?" I asked.

"Of course!" said Grandma. "But don't forget to bring your friends. And bring your pets! There is one more important thing, too. Don't forget to bring your cages, boxes, and leashes!"

Responding

✔ **TARGET SKILL** **Story Structure** What happens in this story? Copy the story map below. Fill in the setting. Then tell about Bernie's problem and how it got solved.

Main characters: Bernie, Mom, Grandma, and friends	Setting: ?
Problem: ? **Solution:** ?	

✎ Write About It

Text to Self Think about a time when you lost something and then found it again. Write a personal narrative paragraph about what happened. Use dialogue to make your narrative come alive.